TUPAC

THE WARRIOR CHIEF

John L. Bowman

Tupac

CONTENTS

CHAPTER ONE
Youth and Challenges

Iknew Tupac growing up and the challenges he faced, and I must tell you he turned out to be quite special. It wasn't always that way; he was rather nondescript in his early childhood—small and scrawny, even a little shy. But there was something different about him that is hard to explain. Unlike the other children, when you talked to Tupac, he listened intently, which I found unnerving. He also seemed designed to move—he was full of energy and always going somewhere to explore or hike. He could be gone for days. But over time what distinguished him most was his keen intelligence—Tupac was always observing and pondering. I followed his dangerous, exciting and prophetic life with great interest, so let me tell Tupac's story to you.

The first time I noticed him was when he was about six. Sometimes children can be quite cruel and single out one person to be the object of derision. In our village it was young Zyanya, who had a deformed arm. She was treated like the runt of the litter because she was small, broken and bent. The other children teased and tormented her unmercifully and called her a monster that never should have been born. Poor little Zyanya could only whimper, cry and struggle to go home. It was sad because she lived in fear, felt rejected and spent her nights shaking and crying—she wanted to die.

I was astounded one day when things changed for her. Unnoticed, I was watching eight-year-old Cualli, the tribe bully, cruelly ridiculing her before pushing her hard and scattering her basket of fruit. She fell and hit her head on a rock, bleeding profusely over one eye and whimpering in a muddied, crumpled mess. I started to walk over to her defense when little six-year-old Tupac took over.

While Cualli was standing over Zyanya with his hand on her small head, normally quiet, reserved Tupac, in a ferocious burst of energy and to everyone's amazement, ran and hit Cualli with surprising force. The impact sent him sprawling backward, airborne. Everyone, including Cualli, was stunned. Cualli got up looking for revenge, somewhat dazed but mostly angry, when Tupac ran at him again and hit him a second time; it again sent him flying. This time Cualli was slow to get up and somewhat disoriented with a new look of fear in his face. I watched as Tupac again advanced, grabbed him by the neck and said in a threatening voice, "Leave Zyanya alone!" Stunned, speechless and shaking, Cualli quickly ran away. Everyone watched in quiet awe and amazement—I heard someone say that it looks like mild, scrawny Tupac is a warrior.

But what happened next was even more remarkable. Tupac then walked over to little Zyanya, knelt down and began quietly gathering her fruits. Then he then put his arm around her, carefully wiped the tears from her eyes and said some things in a low, inaudible voice that made her stop crying and smile. Tupac, now joined by a young girl of the tribe, Yoatl, helped Zyanya to her feet, gave her back her basket full of fruit, took her hands and slowly walked her back to her hut. Nobody, including Cualli, ever bothered Zyanya again.

As the children watched them leave in awe, I heard someone else say that it looks like little Tupac is not only a warrior but also a kind spirit. For any young boy of six years, I must tell you this is a very unusual combination. News of the incident quickly spread around the village, and everyone was amazed at Tupac's courage and kindness. I later learned that when Tupac got home, his parents looked at him quizzically, as they had already heard the story. His mother asked what he had done that day, but he said nothing, ate his dinner and went to bed. I was impressed and thought this young boy just might be the one.

My name is Aztec. I am a longtime member and senior warrior of our village. I was married once but my wife died in childbirth. Without a family of my own, I took up learning the art of being a warrior to protect my village family. I have fought in many fierce battles; I have many scars and am now the leader of the warriors. I am not a learned or articulate man like the priests, but I like to think that I am an honorable, simple and loyal man—and a good judge of character. I love my village and the people in it, but I am worried it may not survive (which I will soon explain). For now, let me continue with Tupac's story and try and tell it to you as best as I can.

Tupac was born into our fading Hidalgo tribe village located in the long, broad caldera of Ceburuco, a long-extinct volcano. It is an isolated and largely safe verdant Garden of Eden with only one narrow entrance, which the ancestors believed could be defended. The village ancestors moved the village there long ago to escape the two main dangers to the tribe that still existed beyond the high cauldron rim. The first were the dreaded occasional puma attacks on our village. The vicious puma is a two-hundred-pound carnivorous cat that can run ompo mile hora[1] and jump eighteen xoxl[2]. Pumas have tremendous fangs and claws that can quickly shred a human. The villagers were most vulnerable when working alone in the fields during the day, but the pumas, being nocturnal, usually hunted at night, each time surprising one or two people and killing them. The villagers lived in great fear of these predators.

Our second danger was more serious. Beyond the rim, the large, fierce Chiapas tribe lived mostly by raiding other villages. Their warriors would come once or twice a year and forcibly take men, women, children and livestock and often burn our huts. With my fellow

---

[1] About fifty miles per hour
[2] About one foot

warriors we fought them repeatedly, but there were too many of them to protect the tribe. These two problems created a kind of paralyzing miasma of fear and impotence in the tribe. To make matters worse, we did not know at the time that there was a far more ominous third challenge to our existence looming in the future.

All this did not seem to bother Tupac much because he was different. He lived by some mysterious transcendent agenda, unaffected by external fear and histrionics. He always had this quiet, calm, enigmatic confidence about him independent of convention and other people. Don't get me wrong, he liked people and was always courteous and respectful, but he was not like others. He usually spoke in a measured and thoughtful way and was always self-possessed. He was always thinking like a profound philosopher. Unbeknownst to us at the time, he was also a born leader. Later in his life he inspired confidence, seemed to know intuitively what to do next and had the will to bring it about. Tupac was not only special and different but also inspirational.

I should mention here that our culture worshiped many gods, one of which was a great warrior whose spirit lived within each of us. This spirit is what makes us strong and brave, and when we are in need, it sometimes appears among us in the form of an exceptional warrior. Although Tupac was too young to be a warrior because of his unusual character, I began to wonder about him.

There was one event I should mention that greatly disturbed Tupac and formed many of his life's later beliefs. One day while playing, he saw the village chief Ati, the village priest and two warriors grab one young boy named Xipil and drag him off scared into the jungle. He was curious so he followed them to an opening, where unobserved he saw them bend whimpering Xipil over a rock, stab his chest with a knife and rip out his heart. Tupac was horrified and wondered why they had done such a brutal thing; from then on was forever wary of the village leaders, priests and especially religion.

Unfortunately for Tupac, our tribe was socially stratified due to Hidalgo tradition, which includes hierarchies. He was born into one of its lower castes, which meant he had a limited future. He was expected to be a field laborer, was barred from marrying above his caste and was never to become a warrior. Young Tupac did not know this at the time, so his childhood was mostly happy and free. As a young boy he loved games, wandered everywhere, built small boats to sail in on the pond and above all played endlessly with the other children of his caste. He spent hours palling around with his best friends Meztil, Izel and Tenoch and playing games with the girls Yaotl, Zuma, Patli and Yaretzi. They would play hide and seek; freely hike the cauldron rim and jungle beyond; swim together in the pond; sing old tribe children's songs; and talk, tease and laugh.

I noticed how over time Tupac and Yoatl became quite fond of each other. He remembered how she had helped him with little Zyanya, how hard and uncomplaining she worked in the fields and how she was always cheerful. He also thought she was the prettiest girl in the village. Yaotl knew Tupac and thought he was rather small and scrawny, but she had always admired his courage and kindness with little Zyanya. I noticed that they would often stay and talk after the other children went home and were always eager to see each other the next day. When Yaotl turned thirteen she began to change. She grew bigger than Tupac, became quieter, lost interest in hiking and swimming and became more focused on her home and family. Tupac noticed that her body was also changing as she developed breasts and broad hips. They both realized what was happening and eagerly talked about a future together. Unfortunately, fate was to change their lives.

Things changed for the worse a few weeks later. It was a cold autumn day and most of us were away hunting game for the winter. Young Tupac was with the women and a few old men harvesting the corn when two young, fearsomely face-painted Chiapas warriors with spears and swords with sharp obsidian blades emerged from the brush, grabbed two women and began dragging them off screaming. The old men with their rakes and furrowers ran to help, and a short, furious fight ensued. They were no match for the Chiapas' youthful strength and well-crafted swords and were losing the fight when Tupac instinctively ran at the biggest warrior and stabbed him in the calf with the sharp end of his hoe. The warrior yelped, dropped the woman, turned and drove his sword through Tupac's shoulder. Surprised, they quickly ran off with one of the women. The face of the warrior who stabbed him became imbedded in Tupac's mind — it was the tribe's fiercest warrior Coyotl, who became his lifelong, deadly enemy.

It had been bloody, and Coyotl killed two of the old, including Tupac's father. With his bloodied shoulder, Tupac cried as he caressed the body of his dead father. The women quietly gathered around and bound Tupac's wound, and the woman he saved kissed him. It was only then Tupac learned that the young woman the Chiapas warriors had taken was Yaotl. Tupac was devastated by losing his father and Yaotl— pain that never left him. He feared for Yaotl's fate, which I will explain shortly.

Tupac eventually recovered from his shoulder wound, and the villagers celebrated him for his bravery in attacking the Chiapas warriors and saving one of the women. He was grateful but quickly became frustrated because the village elders, lead by Chief Ati, refused to elevate him to warrior status. Chief Ati told him that he had helped the village but expected him to continue working in the fields as a laborer because that was his caste. To the chief's displeasure and others' alarm, Tupac told him he had other plans. This was another quality of him I so admired, he was quite self-directed, resilient and not one to wallow in sadness or resentment for long. He buried his father, consoled his mother and Yaotl's parents and began thinking about how to create new weapons that could defeat the pumas and Chiapas. It was about this time I began to believe Tupac really was the one, perhaps part of the spirit, and I quietly started thinking of ways to help him.

CHAPTER TWO

Becoming a Warrior

There are a few things you should know about the society from which the Chiapas and Hidalgo tribes came. The first is that we were a complex hierarchal warrior culture. At seventeen, all young men were expected to begin rigorous military training to learn the art of war and killing. They're expected to become brave, fierce and noble warriors. There were many grades of warriors from the lowly nahuatlor, commoners admitted to this class for special merit; the ocelotl or jaguar class, admitted for bravery; and the highest and most feared cuauhtli or eagle class, reserved for the nobility. Finally, there is the most prestigious class of all warriors, the pipiltin, the cream of the eagle class, consisting of the most important fierce and brave aristocrats. The eagle class's symbol is an eagle on a nopal cactus eating a dove. They worshiped this symbol, but in time I came to consider it evil.

Warriors defended our villages and occasionally hunted, but their main purpose was to capture prisoners. To become a warrior, you had to capture a prisoner, and the more you captured the more you advanced in ranking. To become a jaguar or eagle, for example, you had to capture twenty or more prisoners. The life of a warrior was raiding other villages, constantly fighting and taking prisoners.

The reason warriors captured prisoners was to sacrifice them. We believed the sun god sustained our lives, and if he became displeased, we would all perish. We believed that human sacrifice was essential to please the sun god and allow our lives to continue, so it was our duty to nourish him with human blood. Our job was to just deliver humans to be sacrificed.

This is hard for me to relate, but when a warrior brought in a new prisoner they were either sacrificed or eaten. The lucky ones were quickly taken to the sacred alter and bent backwards over a stone table before they had their beating heart cut out by a priest. I have to pause here because this is so awful, but I must continue. Other prisoners were bound and given to families to eat—we were cannibals. Please give me another moment to gather myself. I know all of this because I am ashamed to admit I was once a Chiapas warrior and I was very good at capturing prisoners for sacrifice—it was an evil practice.

One time I was asked to dinner with a family that had recently received one of my captures. When I got there the family was sitting around chatting with a bound and obviously terrified maybe seventeen-year-old boy. The family had treated him with utmost kindness for days, like one of the family. The women and children had asked him if he was married, whether he had children and what his tribe was like. Shortly after I arrived, the men took him outside and skinned and butchered him, then gave his corpse to the women, who made him into a stew. When they brought the stew in they each took a plate and with bread began eating. One man said Pueblas always taste a little bitter, a woman said he was such a nice boy and one of the children excitedly said he tasted very good.

I was revolted beyond imagination, disgusted to my core, and I decided to leave that bloodthirsty, cruel, evil and inhuman society forever. I quickly left, wandered for some time not knowing my future, and eventually joined the Hidalgo tribe, which is why I am alive to tell this tale today. Tupac knew this about me and my former tribe, which is why he was so despondent when the Chiapas took Yaotl. He knew her possible fates.

The next four years, his late teens, were a period of tremendous growth for Tupac.

His mind improved pondering difficult problems, and with strenuous exercise and arduous hunting trips his body became big, muscular and strong. His natural leadership qualities emerged, and he became the best hunter the tribe had ever seen. He grew into quite a man.

Even though his heritage was as a laborer, like his father, Tupac sought his own destiny. He started working less in the fields and spent more time alone on extended hunts, often gone for weeks. Some elder tribe members lectured him that he was not fulfilling his duty as a laborer to the tribe, but to their displeasure, Tupac just ignored them.

When Tupac was fifteen he said goodbye to his mom and embarked on his first extended hunting trip alone with only a knife, the clothes on his back and a little food. The first thing he had to learn was how to survive in the wild because he quickly became thirsty, cold and hungry when his food ran out. Water was not a problem because it was everywhere, but he had to figure out how to create a shelter from the torrential rains and cold nights. He solved this by leaning some large sticks against a log, covering them with moss and then broad leaves that acted like shingles. Because it got so cold at night, he spent the next day trying to make a fire. After some failures he took a dry piece of bark, carved a notch in the middle, added some dry tinder that he had found in a bird's nest and began vigorously spinning a stick between his hands. It took a while, but to his excitement it smoked and a little fire broke out. The second wet and cold night he was quite warm in his shelter with a glowing warm fire at the entrance.

His biggest problem was finding food. He saw many deer, squirrels, rabbits, peccary and sheep but could never get close enough to kill them. After a week he got so hungry he started eating plants and anything that moved, like worms and slugs. When he returned to the village, he was exhausted, dirty and had no game. The villagers talked skeptically of his hunting prowess, and Ati and some elder members laughed at his station's presumptuousness, which only made Tupac more determined. Even his mother cautioned him about moving outside his caste. She told him that she feared for his safety, to which Tupac responded that he had other plans. She was puzzled but deep down proud of her son.

Tupac's second hunt went a little better. He started studying animal behavior including their tracks. He quietly stalked them and followed their trails to the places they lived. He also learned trapping using the box drop and t-bar snare, which worked pretty well for small game. This time he returned to the village with a few rabbits and a peccary; the villagers were more encouraging, and the elders were more circumspect.

In spite of his challenges, Tupac felt good starting his third hunt, like he was actually achieving something new in life—he was, and this hunt turned out to be the beginning. Much of the hunt was spent thinking about and making weapons not only for hunting but for defeating pumas and Chiapas. The first thing he did was to improve the rudimentary spear he had fashioned on earlier hunts. He found some unusual very hard wood that held an edge, was surprisingly light and could be thrown farther. He practiced long and hard throwing it for distance and accuracy to the point he could throw it a hundred xoxl and have it consistently land within five xoxl of the target. Excitedly he made two more similar spears.

After five days of unsuccessful hunting Tupac was becoming discouraged, but he was determined to get game. On his sixth day, with his growing knowledge of animals and improved stalking ability, he spotted a deer, crept close to it, and quickly threw his spear, which pierced the animal. The ran with his knife and killed it. Tupac stood there looking at his game in happy disbelief, unaware that a puma that had also been stalking that deer, eager to claim it. The puma came charging out of a thicket. Tupac first rose up and screamed at the cat, which kept advancing, then he brandished his knife, which did not seem to scare the cat. Finally he threw his spear when it was seventy-five xoxl out, which landed within four xoxl of the cat and slowed the charge. Tupac threw his second spear at fifty xoxl, which landed within three xoxl, and the cat abruptly stopped and stared at Tupac. Tupac saw fear in its eyes, yanked his last spear from the dead deer, took careful aim, and threw it; it landed within about one xoxl of the cat, who jumped high in the air and ran away. When his heart rate returned to normal, Tupac suddenly realized that he had not only killed a deer but also defeated a puma — he was exhilarated.

That night around his warm fire Tupac again pondered weapons. The puma had not been afraid of him, his scream or his knife, but it was afraid of his spears, which had also killed the deer. He thought about the spears and how they had missed the puma three times, so it occurred to him he needed a weapon with many spears that could fly further and be more accurate. Deep in thought, he recalled the sapling tree he had pushed aside that day hunting that had quickly whipped back and thought about using that tension by bending the sapling in place with some strong vine material. It then occurred to him that to get distance the spear did not need to be so big — he thought just to make it smaller, using the hard wood he used for the spear. With these thoughts, the next day Tupac fashioned a rudimentary bow and small arrow that could be shot quickly and, for long distances, accurately. In the back of his mind he also thought how this new weapon might also work against the Chiapas. It turned out Tupac had invented a new kind of deadly weapon — the bow and arrow. Over time he refined and practiced it and became quite proficient.

This time when Tupac returned from his hunt with a deer, the villagers hailed him as a great hunter, which praise only increased as he hunted more. From then on after hunting he would always return with lots of bigger game including sheep and peccary. He became the best hunter in the village, and Ati and the elders were sullenly silenced.

I had seen enough and decided it was time to help Tupac. I went to him when he was alone and asked to talk. Tupac was surprised because senior warriors rarely talk to field workers but said sure. I said in a low serious voice that quickly got his attention, "Our village is dying because the pumas and Chiapas have caused a culture of fear and defeatism. Every year we lose villagers, and our chief Ati is too weak and fearful to do anything about it. Our village needs a good strong leader, and I think you are that person."

Tupac was surprised. I then said, "I have been watching you closely ever since you were a young boy, and I think you have the character to save us. I have seen your courage and fearlessness, your kindness and humility and your intelligence and ingenuity. Above all, I have seen your natural leadership that draws people to you like a magnet—you inspire confidence. You are a self-directed man who takes his own counsel. You have grown into a powerful, strong man with tremendous athletic ability and skill—the best hunter this village has ever seen. You have all the characteristics to make not only a good warrior but also a chief." I told him that I wanted to teach him to be a warrior. Tupac looked at me long and hard, thinking, and finally said he would be honored.

So our lessons began, and I poured my years of wisdom into Tupac, who absorbed them like a sponge. Unbeknownst to everyone, we spent hours alone together away from the village over the next year working on hand-to-hand combat and boxing skills like jab, cross, hook and uppercut as well as duck, dodge and feint. Then I taught him weapons. I was surprised how good his spear was and how he could throw it so accurately but told him against men you also need a good sword, so I showed him how to make one with a sharp ob-sidian blade. We worked on swordplay and the lunge, parry and riposte. I explained tactics to him, like how to position himself to stab in the most vulnerable places, and mental prepared-ness, like the need to anticipate others' actions by being aware of their body posture and especially watching their eyes. At one time he excitedly showed me his bow and arrow, and I ignorantly said to put that silly thing away.

At the end of every session we would have a contest to practice what I had just taught him. At first I beat him easily, which only made him try harder. I soon learned he was a gifted student, quick to grasp the lesson, quick to execute its movements and adroit at remembering how to use them — plus he had an indomitable, never-give-up spirit so characteristic of great warriors. Between bouts, sweating, exhausted, we would sit and talk about everything but mostly women, love, families and fighting. As we became closer I came to think that there was more going on here than just a teacher instructing a student. After regaining our strength, Tupac would always say "okay, let's get at it!"

As Tupac started mastering his skills, our duels became more intense and often ended in a stalemate. Because he was so strong, fast and smart, it wasn't long before he started beating me. Don't get me wrong, I was trying as hard as I could, but he eventually got so good I always lost and was left wondering if I had just been fighting a man or a spirit. I had seen many good warriors in my time but came to believe Tupac had the makings of the best ever. I took my losses philosophically, thinking I was the father who was inevitably overcome by the powerful son. I can't tell you how proud I was of him.

Near the end of our year I made him a full feathered warrior headdress, told him about body armor and made him a vest of thick quilted cotton that could repulse a spear or sword and covered his torso down to his hips. I painted a black and a red stripe across his forehead and declared him a warrior. I greatly enjoyed this time with Tupac — I think I became the father he lost, and I know he became the son I never had.

CHAPTER THREE

Founding New Village

When Tupac turned eighteen everything changed both for him and the village. Looking back, I think it was a pivotal, momentous time. Tupac was frustrated for many reasons. He was a great hunter but everyone had come to take his ability for granted. He still wanted to be a warrior, but Ati and the village elders would not elevate him. As a young man he was also frustrated because there were no eligible women in the village. All his friends from childhood had married — Zuma had married Meztil, Patli had married Izel and Yaretzi had married Tenoch. All the women were pregnant and were busy starting families. Tupac characteristically kept his frustrations to himself, but I could see that a volcano was brewing, and it violently erupted one fateful day.

The day began with Tupac alone practicing his warrior skills. Suddenly he heard screaming and crying in the distance, grabbed his bow and arrow and ran to the trouble. Most of the villagers were working in the fields when three large, hungry pumas had appeared and quickly killed one villager; they were in the process of mauling two others. Everyone was wildly screaming and waving their arms to scare them away to no avail when Tupac calmly walked out of a thicket and steadily advanced on the cats. The bloody mauling cats stopped and watched him intensely, they were used to villagers running and not advancing. The villagers watched with amazement, thought Tupac was crazy and wondered what the strange contraption he carried was. It was stunned silence all around until

Tupac got within about fifty xoxl of the cats, raised his bow and sent a barrage of deadly arrows into them. Within seconds each puma had an arrow in its gut; they were leaping, writhing and howling at the surprise and pain. Tupac, showing no fear continued to advance pouring another barrage of arrows into the cats, which sent them into more convoluted death throes. When he was within twenty xoxl he unleashed three more fatal arrows into their heads, and they all violently shivered and dropped dead.

Everyone was amazed and began celebrating Tupac for killing the cats and saving them. The joyous men cheered and the adoring women kissed him for his courage and power. They were also curious and somewhat intimidated with his unfamiliar, deadly bow and arrow. I just thought to myself well, I knew Tupac had this in him, but I was surprised with his now not-so-silly contraption. I felt a surge of pride in my progeny.

The chorus of praise continued as the villagers raucously ushered Tupac back to the village, but the atmosphere quickly changed. At first Ati and the elders congratulated Tupac for defeating the pumas, but when the villagers began hailing him as a warrior their faces quickly became dour, defensive and a little angry. Ati said in a slow and artificially deliberate voice, "We naturally appreciate what Tupac had done for us, but our customs do not permit his caste to warrior status." The villagers were stunned and quieted.

I must stop here and explain a little about Ati. He was a short pudgy man who had inherited his status as chief. Unlike his father and grandfather who had been great warriors and leaders, he depended solely on aristocratic tradition to maintain his position. I had never liked him because of this and disdained his arrogant and ineffective leadership. I particularly disliked his supercilious wife Tlalli, who snubbed anyone who did not bow to her artificial superior social status. Personally, I think Ati was jealous and fearful of Tupac's strength and abilities, which is why he stubbornly endeavored to keep him in his place. He used tradition and always wore purple robes as shields for his own weaknesses. But my opinion seems pointless because all this changed when Tupac took the offensive.

For the first time Tupac went face-to-face with Ati, staring him square in the eye. Tupac said forcefully, "I am this tribe's best hunter, I have just alone killed three pumas forever eliminating that threat to our people, and I am a warrior! I deserve to appointed one, and if not, I will leave this village forever!" The last time I had seen Tupac like this was when he defeated the bully Cualli years ago. Ati was initially stunned but quickly recovered and screamed at Tupac that he is forbidden to leave. He ordered three hesitant village warriors to physically detain him. About this time now not-so-little Zyanya ran to Tupac and exclaimed to everyone, "This is no way to treat their best hunter and defender of our village, he should be elevated to warrior statusm and he should be our chief!" This infuriated Ati, who again ordered his warriors to detain Tupac.

When the nervous warriors started advancing Tupac turned, went into his hut and, to everyone's astonishment, emerged in full warrior regalia including an enormous plumed headdress, full cotton breast plate, fearsome sword, spears, bow and arrow and two stripes of black and red paint on his forehead, walked up to one warrior, put his blade to his neck and said without hesitation "I will kill you if I must." Even I was amazed; he looked fearsome—I like to think kind of like me when I was young. The villagers were thrilled, the three warriors were scared to death and quickly retreated and Ati ran away.

So, Tupac left the village forever that day. He first went to his worried mother where they had an emotional goodbye. He said goodbye to all his childhood friends and told them he will miss them, then he thanked crying Zyanya for her support. Finally he came to me and thanked me for teaching him warriorship. He then went to his hut, gathered his meager belongings and left. To be honest, I was not sure what to think — the village had lost its savoir.

It was painful leaving home, but Tupac felt free from village caste custom and alive to new possibilities. He had a vision: a new, better village that would be safe, happy and free from limiting traditions. He spent days first exploring the area outside the caldera for one without luck, so he decided to look inside it further up the valley floor. Nearing its end, he stopped and took a long look at the overgrown rock outcropping they always called the useless high flat place and wondered. He walked over to the base of its smooth twenty-xoxl mostly marble wall and followed it to a small opening where he could climb up to the flat area. It was difficult moving around due to the dense foliage, but he managed to get to the rim and was suddenly overwhelmed with the vista. The broad plain below was large with a stream running through it, which he thought could be perfect for growing crops. He thought defensively that it was a place where he could see anything coming, it was safe because the smooth wall below was difficult to climb and he would be defending the high ground. Excitedly he then walked the surface of the flat place. It was much bigger than he thought, probably a couple of fanega[3], which would make an excellent common area. He looked up and saw that the cliff above hung high overhead covering the back half of the flat area, which would give shelter from the weather. He looked at the cliff walls at the back and imagined hill houses stacked like the Pueblos did in the north. He walked to the back and found many old lava tubes large enough to walk through that went back into the wall and expanded into caverns, and he wondered how they could be used.

Tupac then decided to explore the surrounding area and discovered the field in front was rich soil and fertile for crops, the pond could be used for a variety of purposes like recreation and irrigation and there was plenty of water from the stream. He followed the stream

---

[3] About one acre

up the caldera and discovered its origin was a spring that came directly out of the ground; to his surprise, there was also a nearby hot spring with steaming hot water. He thought that's it, we could pipe cold and hot water in bamboos to the village for cooking, washing and toilets. He imagined hot baths and showers in the caverns for the tired, dirty villagers who had worked in the fields all day. He also found ample building materials like clay for the homes, rocks and some wood. He camped at the rim that night under the stars imagining his future village. In the morning he decided this was the place; he called it Esperanza, or hope.

For the next few months Tupac worked like a man on a mission creating Esperanza. From morning to dusk he worked on clearing the flat top common area of vegetation, working on smoothing rough areas in the wall, clearing the agricultural fields, collecting bamboo for piping water to the caverns, and building a large bath and showers in one cavern and a row of toilets over running water in another. He worked on a rudimentary kitchen in one cavern and prepared another for storage. He built a low, two-xoxl parapet at the top of the wall for safety, sitting and defense; sketched out the locations of paths and homes to be built on the back wall; built a large fire pit in the center of the common area for light, comfort and cooking; and started designing and framing a gate for the opening in the wall.

He also started building his home. There was one place high at the edge of the wall that commanded a tremendous view of both the village and surrounding countryside that he liked. He imagined a couple of simple rooms with a veranda for relaxation and viewing. He made a bed frame of wood, a mattress of straw and animal fur for sheets and covers. After its completion every night Tupac would sit on his veranda happily surveying his village and thinking of the next project—there was so much to do.

While sitting alone at night he often thought of Yaotl. He remembered her cheerfulness, industry and beauty. He would recall their desire to plan a future together and his heart hurt thinking he would never share his new house with her and their children. He shuddered knowing her possible fate, wondered if she was alive, and if so where she was and how she is doing. It was a distressing time for Tupac recalling his lost love.

One day deep in work Tupac was surprised when his old childhood friends showed up. Meztil, Tenoch and Izel along with their wives Zuma, Yaretzi and Patli climbed through the cut, looking at everything with great curiosity. After a joyful reunion of hugging, kissing and laughing Meztil said, "We heard many rumors about what you are doing up here, so we decided to come and see for ourselves." Tupac said, "Wonderful, let me show you my new village, Esperanza" and took them on a grand tour. He described his vision, the wall, the common area and planting area, the location for the houses, and the caverns for bathing, toilets, a kitchen. They then walked down to the pond and up the stream to the spring and hot springs and Tupac explained that the partially built bamboo pipes will send hot and cold water to the village. When they got back to the village the men were giddy with excitement and ideas, and the women were eagerly describing where their houses will be and what they will be like. Tupac took them to the central pot in the middle of the common area where he kept a hodge-podge of stew cooking, and they all sat down for lunch. It felt good for Tupac to back among his old friends.

After much catching up Tenoch said, "Tupac I am amazed by what you have done here. I love it," to which all agreed. Izel then said, "Since you left the village nothing has been the same. People are hungry because there is less game being brought in, many are angry over how Ati and the elders treated you and Ati in his faux-purple has become a little tyrant using the warriors to subdue any disgruntled villagers." Then Zuma exuberantly said, "I love your vision, it is a place of safety where we can raise our children." With that all said they wanted to join and help build Esperanza. So, the next day they returned with all their belongings and went to work building their future together. From there on life got better for Tupac. Within a couple of days his mother arrived with her belongings and said "I am an old woman, I miss my son and I want to do what I can to help my son who has always had other plans." Shortly thereafter Zyanya appeared and told him she wanted to live in a village where he is chief. After that, a steady a stream of the old village members began arriving and were given tours. Everyone was amazed, thought it was a place of safety, hot baths and unheard-of toilets — they all joined.

Tupac's new village was off to a good start.

CHAPTER FOUR
Building Esperanza

Fortune truly does work for the one with a purpose. Tupac's vision had captured the imagination and fired everyone's enthusiasm. They all poured their strength and energy into building Esperanza, working early in the morning until late in the evening. Nobody worked harder than busy Zyanya, who became a source of inspiration. It was an exciting time because it was a new beginning for a cherished common purpose. Everyone was busy and happy.

There was much to do, so they broke into units, each focused on building a part of the new village. Some worked on the common area or yard; others on the long, low parapet and central fire pit; and still others in the caverns shaping the tub, toilets and kitchen. They worked closely with those building the piping system for running hot and cold water that was brought down through bamboo pipes from the hot and cold springs above. Some started excavating for walkways and framing for stacked houses on the back wall, and Tupac started building a small apartment for his mother, who was thrilled.

Outside the forming village those with lapidary skills worked on the face of the slippery wall and others started building a stout entrance gate at the opening. Most started clearing and planting crops in the fields including maize, chili, beans, squash, tomatoes and avocados. They decided to expand the size of the pond with a dam so more water would be available for irrigation and recreation. They even created a small grassy park on the shoreline for play and swimming. Beyond the fields some started building rudimentary stables for the animals including pigs, chickens, sheep and cows.

Tupac turned out to be the outstanding leader I always knew he was. He always listened intently, asked questions, weighed pros and cons, consulted others and then made decisions. His decisions were never imperious commands but rather suggestions, which carried such weight they were unquestioningly obeyed. He became the unacknowledged, revered chief of the tribe.

After a couple of years of hard work the village was almost done. It was a sight to behold — it looked like a God-created shining city of hope on a high hill — it was a jewel in the jungle. There was still much to do, like the massive entrance gate, but most of the infrastructure was done. The walls were done, many homes had been completed and the fields were producing bumper crops of maize, beans, squash and tomatoes. Along with game from hunting there was a bounty of food for all, and the large pot of rich stew was always full in the yard.

One event in particular became the story villagers loved to retell; it eventually became a legend. The day the baths, showers and toilets were completed everyone left their work and came to watch in excitement and anticipation. The spigots were opened and the large swimming pool-sized bath began filling with hot steamy water. When it was full giddy villagers unabashedly shed their clothes, got in and soaked — they could not believe the luxury of it all. Others cautiously took showers carefully adjusting the hot and cold valves for the right temperature and many tried the unheard of toilets with running water below. For them this was like heaven.

The houses turned out to be quite comfortable. Shielded from the elements by the overhanging cliff, most homes consisted of two rooms: one for living and the other for sleeping. They were clean, dry and private. Tupac's mother liked her apartment so much she wove a rug for the floor incorporating a dove holding and olive branch as a symbol of hope, courage and safety. She showed it to Tupac and said, "Our legacy has it that one of our ancestors lost at sea was visited by a dove with an olive branch signifying land and safety were nearby." Tupac looked at his mother's symbol and said he liked it but added, "You know, Mom, peace only comes through strength and courage that brings safety." He suggested she add an eagle to the rug with one wing behind the dove symbolizing courage and strength's defense of peace and safety and his mother exclaimed, "Of course!" She rewove the rug, which became Esperanza's emblem, and with that the old traditional evil warrior eagle symbol was transformed into a good protector of peace and safety. Everyone liked it so much his mother decided every house should have one, so she recruited a few other women, and they began weaving rugs for all the homes.

As word about Esperanza spread many more people from other villages trickled in who, amazed, invariably joined; the village grew even more. One day Tupac, along with Meztil, Tenoch and Izel, who had become the ruling council, stopped and surveyed their creation. They saw happy villagers whose former malaise and defeatism had vanished, now replaced with courage, energy and hope. They observed how prosperous and clean it looked and took particular satisfaction in knowing that it had been designed for safety. Little did they know at the time, Esperanza's defenses would soon be seriously challenged.

It was about this time when my life changed for the better. I was out hunting one day alone when, unobserved, I saw Tupac, also hunting, and three Chiapas warriors ominously following him. I silently followed them for a while when suddenly the warriors attacked Tupac and a violent sword fight began, one against three. I watched with admiration as my student-son defended himself admirably — with satisfaction I thought I had done a good job teaching him warriorship. After a minute or so I calmly walked up behind the three Chiapas and asked Tupac if he would like any assistance. The warriors turned, stunned. Tupac said it would be appreciated, and after a few furious parries and thrusts we quickly dispatched two of them and the third ran away. Afterward we laughed, hugged and said what a grand fight it had been. It was a special fight for me because for the first time in my life I felt like I was fighting alongside my kin. My soul was touched when Tupac said, "nice parries, Dad." Tupac then asked me to join his new village as one of the ruling council, and I said yes. I was thrilled with the opportunity to be a senior warrior in the ruling council for a new vibrant village with an outstanding leader. I went straight back to the old village, collected my belongings and was enthusiastically welcomed to the new village when I arrived that evening.

At my first council meeting my expectations were somewhat dampened when Tupac told us he wanted us to learn how to use the bow and arrow. I thought good grief, I have to learn how to use that silly toy, but reluctantly we all agreed. Tupac showed us how to build it, what material to use, how to string it and how to shoot it. He asked us each to make one along with twenty arrows and practice to the point where we could hit a target the size of a watermelon at fifty xoxl. This we all did, and I must say I got pretty good at the little contraption.

The end of the old village abruptly happened one day a little later that year when all of the remaining villagers showed up and asked to join. Tupac was away hunting when they arrived. The group was led by Ati, dressed in his purple robe, who imperiously demanded to be the chief of the new village. He said tradition required he be chief and began issuing orders including one to build a house for him and his supercilious wife Tlalli. Shortly Tupac showed up, quickly sized up the situation, approached nervous Ati, put his sword to his throat and said, "Get out!" Ati hesitated briefly. Tupac inched his blade into his neck. Ati shuddered, turned and ran away. Ati's wife Tlalli pleaded to stay.

One of Tupac's great characteristics was clemency, so after a minute he said, "This village is a meritocracy; there is no aristocracy here. If you do your part and work you are welcome, but if I ever hear of any pretension to royalty I will kick you out." Tlalli quietly nodded, and with those simple words and gestures, one tradition ended and a new, brighter era began. Ati's remains were found a few months later beyond the rim. He was apparently killed by pumas.

CHAPTER FIVE

Puma attack

It was a joy living in Esperanza—it was so different from the old village. Everyone was busy, happy and thriving. I spent most of my time out hunting, usually with some of the other warriors, to help feed the village. It was on one hunt with Tupac and Tenoch that we heard a different kind of animal snorting and rustling in the distance. Thinking it was game, we went to see. To our amazement at a clearing we saw four or five of the strangest animals totally unfamiliar to us. They were huge, four-legged stocky animals with long bodies and heads, bushy manes and tails and spotty coloring. We did not know if they were dangerous but showed ourselves anyhow and prepared for a fight, but they just stood there peacefully and whinnied at us. Warily we approached them, but to our surprise they quickly came to us—they obviously had been tamed somehow. We carefully stroked their rather course hair, which seemed to please them. Not knowing what to do next, we took some vine and made ropes, which we put around their necks, and we led them to our camp for the night. We learned later that these were Choctaw horses that the foreigners called Spaniards had brought to our land; they were strong and brave animals with great stamina, and they had been used mostly for warfare.

That night around the fire we talked about what to do with these new creatures. Tupac said if we could learn to ride them they could carry us long distances quickly and they might be useful in defense of Esperanza. So the next day Tupac gingerly mounted one and to our amazement awkwardly rode around. The rest of us did the same and soon we were all giddy trotting around our campsite on these strange beasts. They were clearly tractable animals, but we did not know how to direct them until Tupac noticed how sensitive their mouths were. He fashioned a kind of bridle made of a stick and vine that we put into their mouths to direct them. By the end of the day we were galloping, turning and backing up these wonderful animals like experts — it was really fun. I thought to myself that I like being around Tupac because there is always something new and exciting going on, unlike the old village.

The villagers were astonished, some scared and others really curious the next day when the three of us confidently rode our horses in stringing two behind — they had never seen such a sight — they had a lot of questions we could not answer. Over time they got used to them and they became an integral part of the village. Many of the young girls started taking care of them and they bucked off many of the showoff young boys. We started growing the hay they liked to eat, built stables by the animal barns and would sometimes use them for plowing and hauling. At Tupac's suggestion, the five village warriors learned how to ride and gradually perfected a war attack. We first practiced charging the enemy, then shooting our arrows at a distance and finally when upon them slashing with our swords. It was a coordinated charge on horses at which we became quite proficient. It also turned out we had both males and females that began producing many spirited colts.

No sooner had the village become accustomed to the horses that the first great threat to Esperanza occurred. It was late in the day and most villagers were still in the fields when someone excitedly ran in, quickly climbed to the parapet and began loudly ringing the warning bell yelling "Pumas! Pumas! Pumas!" Without hesitation everyone immediately ran for the safety of the village, we ran for our bows and a few people barricaded the unfinished gate with some timber after the last one stumbled in. Within minutes we saw about eight pumas stealthily advancing on our walls obviously looking for the victims they did not find at the old long-abandoned village. We were surprised there were so many because they usually hunt alone or in pairs. We were concerned they might be able to leap our wall.

The atmosphere of fear was palpable, but Tupac was brave and resolute. With the entire village watching he got us warriors together on the parapet and said, "I know our arrows can kill these cats because I have done it. I want to end this puma threat now, so shoot to kill and keep shooting until your run out of arrows." We lined up, loaded our bows, pulled them taught, and took deadly aim; when the pumas were within fifty xoxl Tupac yelled, "Fire!" Hit with a fusillade of arrows, the stunned pumas leaped and writhed as the arrows pierced their necks, chests, legs and heads. We quickly poured volley after volley into the cats—about seventy-five rounds until Tupac said, "Stop!" When the dust cleared all we saw were eight very dead bloody pumas. A spontaneous cheer of joy went up from the astounded villagers, and with that the puma threat to the village ended forever. It had been a short, furious, one-sided fight, and we were elated until Tupac reminded us the Chiapas would be far more dangerous. Afterward we had a feast to celebrate our victory and ate puma meat for the next month. I was pleasantly surprised that Tupac's little contraption worked so well—I expected nothing less from a spirit.

After that the village lived in peace for a year or so despite rumors that the Chiapas were planning to attack. We spent much of the time finishing the massive gate, building more houses for new members and creating a central cooking kitchen. We moved the yard pot to one large cavern that was open on one side so the fumes could escape, built ovens and added tables and benches. There were also a few smaller side caverns where we stored food. With its always-cooking pot of stew, along with the bath, the kitchen became one of the social centers of the village. Near its completion Esperanza was safe and comfortable — and I think the finest village in all our land.

Tupac had more in mind, and I don't think it is an exaggeration to say about this time he started a cultural revolution. I am old school and had lived my life according to tradition, but Tupac changed much of that. I was not comfortable with much of it at first but over time came to understand, appreciate and accept much of his vision of a good society. The first change was regarding tradition, castes and work. Our Hidalgo tribe had always been a stratified society with the lower castes doing most of the manual labor like cooking, tending the fields and taking care of the animals. Tupac asked why it would not be better to let everyone choose their own job based on talent and inclination. With that Tenoch's wife Yaretzi, who had always been a wife and mother, jumped up and said, "I love my family, but I always wanted to be a builder!" So, the next day she went and started working on finishing the massive gate to Esperanza. It was amazing; she created a large self-latching lock and impressive symbol of the eagle and dove over the gate. Everyone was amazed, so we tried Tupac's suggestion, and the villagers not only became eager to do their jobs, but what they did was done far better.

Tupac started asking why we always had an authoritarian, top-down chiefdom government. He asked why we should not reverse it, with authority coming from the bottom up; a system that derives its authority from everyone. This caused quite a stir because everyone wanted Tupac to remain as chief. Tupac thought for a bit and then said, "Okay, but only on the condition you can vote me out anytime." Reluctantly we started voting and creating unheard of principles like the rule of law and equal treatment under the law. The village also embraced a meritocracy where strengths were encouraged to flourish and be rewarded. It was interesting watching how these changes affected Ati's ex-wife, the once arrogant Tlalli. I notice that over time she became one of the hardest working, most productive, helpful and well-liked citizens. I came to the conclusion that Tupac was right to eliminate the customs that made bad people.

One day Tupac, who was not inclined to superstition, led a lively village discussion on whether to change the village religion. The old religion had been brutal. We had believed in many gods that represented parts of reality we did not understand. One such superstitious belief was that we are living in the era of the fifth sun and the world could end violently anytime. In order to postpone our destruction and appease the gods, other villages had performed human sacrifices. We thought that if we fed the gods human blood the sun would keep us alive. While the villagers were debating what gods to worship Tupac stood up and, obviously agitated, said, "When I was a young boy I watched the village priest murder an innocent young boy one day because of the damn gods!" This quickly silenced everyone because they had all lived their lives in fear of being sacrificed. Tupac continued, "It is an ugly, disgusting and inhuman act that will never occur again as long as I am chief!" I sensed a collective sigh of relief that an old, brutal and feared religious tradition suddenly was no more.

He then said, "Why not worship eternal and bountiful nature as a deity without our unrealistic human expectations?" With quiet reverence everyone agreed, and with that the Hidalgo tribe's religion became pantheistic and priests were replaced by wise philosophers who were called Sabiduria. Tupac had forever replaced a cold, menacing and uncaring religion with a warm, humanistic one, and his star rose a little higher.

So far I had been willing to at least try Tupac's new ideas, but this ended when he started talking about the role of women. Because women were smaller and weaker they had always been subservient to men, and because of their unique reproductive and nurturing abilities, they were always relegated to the role of mother, raising children and preparing food while usually working in the fields. Indeed, because the village had become so vibrant most of the young ones were pregnant and gloriously overwhelming the village with new children. But at one village meeting Tupac said, "We all have strengths and weaknesses, so why not allow women to choose what they want to do?" He said, "They have the same basic body and the same reason as men, so why not treat them equally and allow them to fill other roles?" Then out of the blue crippled Zyanya jumped to her feet and blurted out, "*I want to be a warrior!*" For the first time I saw Tupac at a loss for words. I thought this time he has gone too far and left the meeting.

I was angry with Tupac for a few days and eventually went and told him his view of women was wrong. I said that I may be an older man set in my ways, but women have always had a specific role in society that he was ignorantly abandoning. I asked him who was going to raise the children and cook our food if the women stop doing it? Tupac was obviously concerned but said nothing, so I left, still angry.

Tupac was in a dilemma and asked Zyanya how she could become a warrior. Zyanya hesitated and then said she could get good at the bow and arrow. Tupac thought a bit and said we do need someone who can shoot the arrow far and accurately, kind of like a sniper. Everyone thought it was preposterous that crippled Zyanya could shoot an arrow and become a village warrior, but we went along assuming nothing would come of it.

Somewhat skeptical Tupac spent the next few months working with Zyanya teaching her archery. He made her a bow that could shoot long distances and experimented with different woods including bamboo and birch, but he soon discovered that wood from the Osage orange tree was the best because it was durable and stiff but still flexible enough to bend. He also made the bow longer for more torque. Unbeknownst to us Zyanya later added a wood projection stabilizer to the bow so it would not waver after shooting for accuracy. Finally he and Zyanya crafted a very strange looking rest that fit her deformed arm perfectly and surprisingly added more stability. Zyanya was thrilled, and after Tupac had taught her more basics, she spent days away from the village working to strengthen her deformed arm and body and determinedly practicing archery.

I think it was about six months later when Zyanya announced that she wanted to show everyone how she could shoot. The next day we all went to the fields to humor little Zyanya, who had set up some targets. Tupac had told the warriors he wanted us to be able to hit a watermelon at fifty xoxl, which was our limit. Zyanya loaded an arrow, pulled her strange looking bow taught, took careful aim and hit a target the size of a grape at sixty xoxl! She then loaded another arrow, took aim and nailed a tomato at 120 xoxl! With our mouths agape she loaded another and hit a cantaloupe at 180 xoxl! Tenoch had once been able to shoot an arrow an incredible 150 xoxl, so when Zyanya loaded her last arrow and shot it four hundred xoxl, everyone was utterly speechless! It turned out we were amateurs and she was best bow-woman in the village.

Little deformed and bullied Zyanya who had lived her life ashamed of her deformity and struggling to just be normal was elated. She beamed with well-earned pride when the villagers began cheering her new ability. She felt a surge of inner strength and a new sense of worthiness. She could not believe she was being hailed for a physical prowess she had achieved and alone possessed. Tupac smiled, we immediately accepted her into the warrior class, and I was so amazed my attitude about the female sex changed forever. I went to Tupac and said, "After watching Zyanya perform, I now think you were right: women should have more freedom to pursue their inclinations, hell I can't have babies, but if more women can shoot like Zyanya I'll sure do the cooking!" Tupac just put his hand on my shoulder and said, "Don't worry Aztec — you are a far better warrior than cook."

A few days later Zyanya dropped another bombshell on Tupac although this time it was ironic. She asked him if they could talk in private and when alone that she had fallen in love with Cualli, her former bully. She said he had changed, had grown up and now treated her with great kindness and respect. She said he had been courting her for some time and recently asked her to marry him. She said she wanted to but was worried about bearing a deformed child, so she asked Tupac's opinion. Tupac's first thought was about the irony of the once mean bully now becoming the spouse of the warrior he once abused. Amused Tupac thought a little more and said, "Zyanya you have been one of my loyalist defenders over the years and I want you to be happy." He said he thought the chance of a deformed child was low because her family did not have a legacy of deformity. He then said, "By all means, if you truly love that bully marry him, have children and be happy." Feeling suddenly free from the past, Zyanya cried, hugged Tupac, married

Cualli a few months later and eventually gave birth to many perfectly formed children.

I am a proud warrior not used to humbling myself to anyone, but I had done so with Tupac and now in honesty I did it with another. This is not easy for me. Ever since Ati's arrogant wife Tlalli had joined the village I had treated her with disdain, which she always endured in silence. One day I noticed her coming in after working in the fields all day, dirty and exhausted but cheerfully helping one young mother carry her crops and children. While watching her I got flashbacks of her on her knees scrubbing the toilets, sweating in the kitchen preparing food and always cheerful. I flashed again on how other people had been drawn to her strong, happy personality and began wondering if my judgment of her had been wrong.

After she showered I approached her and asked "Tlalli, may I talk with you?" Startled, perhaps a little fearful and hesitant and after a long silence she said, "Yes." We went and sat on the parapet and I said, "Tlalli I have held a poor opinion of you and have treated you badly ever since you joined the village." She smiled at me quizzically. Embarrassed and faltering, I then asked her if we could begin again, and she said she would like that. With that we had a long conversation about Tupac, Esperanza and her former husband Ati and reminisced about the old village. I told her about my dead wife and child. She said she was sorry about my wife and child. She had heard about my changed views on women and was impressed. She also said that she was flattered a senior warrior like me wanted to talk with her. While she was talking I began to realize she was not what I had thought she was at all, saw how handsome a woman she was and began seeing her through new eyes. I humbled myself and my spirit soared.

CHAPTER SIX

Spaniard

Terrified Yaotl was bound, blindfolded and roughly taken to the Chiapas village after being captured by warriors in the old village. Coyotl and the elders along with Coyotl's scheming sorceress mother Coaxoch debated what to do with her. They would usually take enemy prisoners directly to the altar and sacrifice them to the gods or eat them, but Coaxoch had a different idea. She said because of Yaotl's bearing she must be a princess and reminded everyone that their important festival

Xiuhmolpilli was to occur in thirteen years. This was a special festival that was celebrated every fifty-two years in order to prevent the world coming to an end. Coaxoch said that if they sacrificed a princess the gods would be very pleased. As an afterthought she said that the gods also preferred virgin sacrifices so she should never be violated — she must be pure so they do not end the world. Everyone agreed, so poor Yaotl's fate was sealed — she was made a slave and forced to toil from morning to night doing all the dirty, hard and miserable jobs while awaiting her death.

Yaotl's life became one of verbal abuse, subjection and solitude. She felt dead, but the thought of Tupac always made her happy. When alone in the evenings she would recall his fading face with joy. She remembered his courage, kindness with little Zyanya and their life plans together. She wondered where he was and what he was doing. Her sadness at one point turned to terror when she surmised she was to be sacrificed, but she gradually resigned herself to her fate. It was only her love for Tupac that brought the hope that kept her spirit alive.

It was around this time that we started hearing rumors about foreign invaders to our lands that rode horses, wore bright metal armor and had a strange weapon that made a loud crack and could kill at long distances. We learned that they had been raiding villages, terrifying and subjugating the people and stealing. Tupac was concerned but thought with Esperanza's defenses, our bow and arrows and ability to ride horses, we could defend ourselves. Within a few days his view quickly changed.

Tupac and I were hunting when we saw two of these strange men. One was white with shiny armor and a long stick and the other smaller and dark skinned. We decided to follow them when the big one saw a deer probably a hundred xoxl's away in a thicket, raised his stick and with a loud bang and puff of smoke instantly killed it. I gasped with amazement, which they heard. The white man quickly reloaded his weapon and aimed it at us. The instant it went bang I felt a sting in my thigh and fell to the ground bleeding. Tupac quickly fired an arrow at the man but it harmlessly bounced off his breast plate. He continued to reload his gun, so Tupac charged him, and they got into a furious sword fight. Tupac's sword could not pierce his armor so he sliced his bare leg and drove his sword into his neck, killing him. Tupac then turned on the dark skinned man who was cowering in fear.

It became clear the man was no threat so Tupac asked who he, was but the man could only mumble in fear. He bound the man's hands and brought him back to see how I was. It turned out to be a flesh wound, which we put healing oregano on and bound. Nearby we set up camp for the evening and started asking our captive questions. His fear gradually faded and he said his name was Nacalli, but his masters called him Diego. He said he was a mestizaje, or an ethnic mix of Spanish and native, that he had been made a slave by the Spanish and wanted to escape because he was treated harshly. We were interested because this is the first time we had heard the new invaders' name. We decided he was harmless, so we told him about ourselves and Esperanza. Nacalli got excited and said he wanted to go with us to our village, so the next morning we broke camp and went home with the Spaniard's fire stick and Nacalli leading his donkey laden with his belongings.

Tupac was concerned his arrow had been ineffective against our new threat the Spaniards. He thought with their armor and fire stick we could be easily defeated. He started asking Nacalli lots of questions and learned the fire stick was called an arquebus that fired little balls using gun powder that was ignited by flint, none of which Tupac understood. Nacalli also said only these balls can pierce the Spaniards armor. With that Tupac decided he had to learn how to fire the arquebus and asked Nacalli to teach him; he agreed.

Nacalli spent much time with Tupac over the next few days teaching him everything about the arquebus. He explained the stock, trigger, barrel, breach, priming pan, ball, ram rod and touch hole. He described gunpowder, flint and how the explosion in the barrel propels the ball. Tupac was amazed and said, "Teach me how to fire it." Nacalli showed how to add gunpowder to the barrel, insert the ball, ram it tight, strike the flint in the priming pan, light the fuse aim and hold on for dear life because it has a tremendous kick when it goes off.

A few days later they went off a ways from the village to see if Tupac could fire it. Nacalli put an apple on a rock about a hundred xoxl out, Tupac loaded it and lifted the long, heavy and ungainly gun, aimed it, lit the fuse, waited only a few seconds. It went off with a deafening bang that wrenched Tupac's shoulder and exploded the apple. Tupac was amazed and practiced more shots to hone his ability. On the way back to the village, always thinking Tupac said one problem is where will be get the gunpowder, bullets and flints to use it, to which Nacalli laughed and said he had brought three huge sacks of them on his donkey. Tupac was relieved but began thinking that the gun might be ineffective against the Spaniards because it took almost thirty seconds to reload, which would mean only two rounds per minute. He thought any battle could be over after ten rounds and started thinking of ways to make the gun fire faster.

It turned out Nacalli loved Esperanza. He liked the people, the freedom and especially the baths and showers. He asked us if he could join and the village happily accepted him. Over time he became Esperanza's blacksmith shoeing the horses and turning out ironworks, which was something we had never known before.

Tupac decided we needed an extra layer of defense against these formidable Spaniards so at the next village meeting he said he thought we should build a wall at the entrance to the caldera. The entrance was a deep V shape with a narrow bottom, perhaps fifteen xoxl wide at the bottom, thirty at the top and about fifty xoxl high. He said a stout gate could be at the bottom, the wall should be made of stone with a smooth front and parapet at the top for shooting. The villagers discussed the idea and agreed, and Tlacelel the best stonemason in the tribe, enthusiastically said he would take charge of building it. He collected a gang of men and started the next morning on the wall.

As usual Tupac was always thinking, leading and working, but over time I noticed a strange sadness descend on him. He seemed to grow quieter, less decisive and more distant. In the evenings he began withdrawing from everyone, sitting on his high veranda staring into space. I asked him what was wrong, and he only evaded my question. His old friends noticed this also and became concerned. Izel suggested they all get together to discuss ways to figure this out. He said that because I was one of his best friends and Zyanya his most loyal supporter we should join them. We met secretly outside the village and discussed the problem for some time when Zuma, who had been uncharacteristically quiet during the talk, jumped up and said "I know why he is sad — it is so obvious."

Everyone went quiet and listened. Zuma said, "He misses Yaotl and there are no women in the village that can replace her. He sees his future without a woman he loves, with no intimacy with a woman and with no children or family." Then Zuma said, "I have an idea," and we began hatching a plan.

My role was to bring Tupac to a meeting, which I did. He was a little hesitant not knowing for sure where we were going but humored me. I led him to the others, where he was surprised to see all his old friends gathered together with such serious faces. I asked him to sit down and went to a side to watch. First Patli got up and said, "Tupac you are unhappy because Yaotl is gone and you have no woman or family." Then Yaretzi stood and said, "We all love you and have a plan to help. Long ago the Hidalgo tribe had a tradition of polygamy, and we have decided to temporarily bring it back for you." Then Zuma stood and said "Patli, Yaretzi and I along with our husbands have decided to share us three women with you as your wives."

Stunned Tupac looked at Metzil, Tenoch and Izel who only smiled with approval. Zuma then said, "We love you, we want you to be happy so we want to share your bed and have your children." With that excited Zyanya jumped up and said, "I don't care what Cualli says, me too!"

Tupac was stunned—it was the only time I ever saw a tear in his eye. After gathering himself he said slowly that he was a very lucky man to have such good friends and that they were right—he did long for Yaotl and wanted a woman, children and family. But then smiling said, "Thanks for the offer but I must decline—I would never feel right interfering with your families—with your marriages and children. Please don't worry, I will be okay," and heartily hugged everyone including me.

I am not a sentimental man but when Tupac hugged me I felt an emotional surge. I think it was because it was not only my adopted son showing affection but perhaps a spirit from the past. I was so affected that later I asked him about the warrior spirit. He looked at me for a long time and said, "Aztec, I really don't know, but sometimes I do feel like I am living some eternal life, a warrior life. When Chief Ati denied me warrior status something in me just would not allow it—I just felt I had a different destiny. I can't explain it." This answered many of my doubts.

CHAPTER SEVEN

Tribe attack

After our meeting Tupac seemed to regain a little of his natural vigor. The people of Esperanza began enjoying the fruits of their labors—a kind of halcyon time. After a hard day's work they took long hot showers or soaked in the bath and on warm days many would go to the grassy park on the pond and relax and swim. Little did we know that we were about to endure the second and most serious threat to our existence and Tupac's greatest challenge as a warrior.

It began about midday when most everyone was working when suddenly the same villager who had warned us of the pumas ran in panting and sweating, climbed to the parapet and began furiously ringing the warning bell screaming "Chiapas, Chiapas, Chiapas!!" The village flew into action; people in the fields immediately dropped their tools and ran for the gate, Metzil and Izel ran to the stables and quickly brought the horses in at full gallop, Tenoch and I ran and collected the bows and arrows, swift Camaxtli and Millintica ran out to quickly survey the enemy and Zyanya climbed to Tupac's high veranda with her weapon. Within minutes everyone, including Camaxtli and Millintica, who got back just in time, were inside the finished gate, which Tupac and a few others closed and latched solidly thanks to Yaretzi's new latch. Unfortunately the arquebus would be of no help because it had been dismantled.

It did not take long for about twenty-five heavily armed Chiapas warriors painted in ominous war colors lead by Coyotl to arrive. As everyone hid behind the parapet, obviously surprised Coyotl said in a taunting, sarcastic voice "Well, it looks like the Hidalgo tribe has abandoned their old village and built a new one with a little wall. You must be quite afraid of us to have gone to such effort." While he was speaking, six of his warriors slinked off to his left looking for a way to scale the wall, and Camaxtli and Millintica followed them in case they did.

Tupac knew his enemy Cotoyl well; he was used to villagers cowering before him in fear. He wanted to play on his complacent arrogance so he had recruited the village's oldest and most feeble man, Millintica. Tupac explained the situation and told Millintica he wanted him to stand and talk with them so Cotoyl would think they were feeble. Tupac also told Millintica it would be dangerous and he could get killed, to which Millintica said he would be honored to risk his life for Esperanza. With this Millintica showed himself and in an old wavering voice said, "We are a peaceful people who intend you no harm" and then asked what they wanted in order to leave us alone. Emboldened, Coyotl said "I am here because you killed two of my warriors and we want revenge. We are going to kill your men including that traitor Aztec, take all of your women and property and destroy your village." He laughed menacingly, threw his spear at Millintica, which missed him by much less than an xoxl, and yelled "Attack!" With that the Chiapas started throwing a hail of spears at us, and the epic battle for Esperanza began.

To Coyotl's utter surprise, Tupac, Meztil, Tenoch, Izel and myself with faces painted for war showed ourselves and sent a hail of arrows, a weapon they had never seen, into their mist quickly wounding and killing many. With spears flying by our heads we resolutely kept up our barrage of arrows helped by Zyanya who was high on the veranda methodically pouring round after round of deadly accurate arrows into the Chiapas, who had no idea where they were coming from. Many villagers got into the fray and started throwing anything they could at the Chiapas. Just then the six Chiapas warriors who had shimmied up a pole poured over the parapet to our right and started sword fighting with Camaxtli and Millintica, who were outnumbered. While Meztil, Tenoch, Izel and Zyanya kept up the barrage of arrows, Tupac and I ran over to help them in a furious fight. Swords were flashing, flesh was being cut and blood was flowing.

At about this time it looked like we were losing when a few Chiapas were able to scale the front of the wall and the fighting became hand to hand, Tenoch went down with a spear in his neck and Millintica was killed with a stab to the stomach. I must pause here because it was at precisely this point when Tupac's spirit emerged and saved Esperanza. He suddenly turned into this invincible, fierce Spartan warrior god from the ages—it was like he transformed into the spirit of the finest warrior fighting machine and just went wild. Screaming, his sword flew and he quickly killed three warriors; I killed two more, and Camaxtli along with many villagers attacked the last one. Tupac yelled "Come with me" to me and Meztil, and we turned and ran leaving Izel and the villagers to fight the few remaining warriors on the parapet. We quickly mounted our horses and flew through the gate and charged the remaining Chiapas. They had never seen horses and were stunned when the three of us galloped at them at full speed shooting our arrows and plowing through them with slashing swords. Tupac quickly dismounted and went straight for surprised and now frightened Coyotl. They got into an epic sword fight with both slashing and parrying to kill. At one point Coyotl stabbed Tupac in the shoulder—the same place he had done it twenty years earlier. Tupac momentarily wavered but this time he was too big and strong. He said, "You killed my father and took my Yaotl" then quickly knocked Coyotl off his feet and forcefully stabbed him in the heart, killing him.

It was over as quickly as it had begun. Amongst the carnage of dead Chiapas bodies a great spontaneous cheer went up. We had won a great battle. Every one of the Chiapas warriors had been killed even though we had lost Millintica and a few brave citizens, Tenoch was seriously injured and Tupac was bleeding. But with our victory the Chiapas threat vanished forever, which the village joyously celebrated that night. Tenoch and Tupac eventually recovered from their wounds. A solemn funeral was later held for Millintica, and Camaxtli, Tupac and I became protectors of his wife and children for support and to help raise them well.

Later that night I saw Tupac comforting dead Millintica's crying wife and children, and I again saw the unique combination of kindness and courage I had first seen in him many years ago in his youth. It then became clear after recalling his sudden surge of primordial spiritual warrior energy that had saved us he truly was a warrior spirit from the past. He had become not only the best warrior I had ever known but in my opinion had joined the ranks of the best warriors of all time.

CHAPTER EIGHT
Chiapas Village

In spite of Tupac's shoulder wound, early the next morning he, Metzil, Izel, Camaxtli and I went on horseback to the Chiapas village while the villagers buried the dead and tended to Tenoch. The Chiapas were quite intimidated seeing us five Hidalgo warriors on horseback with red and black painted foreheads armed with bows, arrows and swords confidently ride in. There were about seventy of them, mostly women, children, old men and a few adolescent males. Tupac rode up to them and said, "Your warriors attacked our village yesterday, so we killed them, all including Coyotl your chief." With that a hush of fear filled the air, and there was a scream from one haggard old woman at the back.

We learned later that this old woman's name was Coaxoch; she was Coyotl's mother and the real evil source of our troubles. She had been the one coaching her son and his warriors to harass other villages. She told them to steal other tribes' women and property, and she was the one who sacrificed prisoners or sent them to a pot of stew in order to appease the gods and gain power. She was furious that Tupac had killed her son, and she quickly raised a blowpipe and shot a poison dart at Tupac, which bounced off his cotton breastplate. As she was loading a second dart Tupac quickly demounted, drew his sword and raced after her in the crowd. She ran and then turned and hissed at him preparing to shoot her second dart when Tupac deftly swung his sword and instantly beheaded her. It is hard to describe everyone's reaction, but I sensed a collective sigh of relief that the evil dove-eater had been dispatched.

Tupac then mounted his horse and told the Chiapas that they will no longer threaten our tribe and must leave not only their village but the area within two days. He said, "You may leave in peace, but we will return in three days and kill anyone who has remained. It was at this moment Tupac happened to see a lone figure at the back of the crowd with a sack over their head. Disgusted with cruelty he asked the hushed crowd who it was but got no answer. He rode over to them, reached down and yanked the sack off their head. It was a startled young woman who had never seen a horse. Tupac stared at her in silence, then he dismounted and took her trembling hand. "Yaotl?" The young woman looked at Tupac and said, "Tupac?" It was really her!

In spite of being mistreated and rather disheveled, Yaotl was still a beauty. Yaotl looked at Tupac, who she remembered as small and scrawny, with admiration and joy. He was now big and strong. It had been thirteen years since they had seen each other, so for a long time they embraced in silence. I looked on with a smile because I was so happy that Tupac had found his long lost love. Finally, Izel went to hopelessly and emotionally distracted Tupac and said that we should get going. Tupac mounted and held his hand out to Yaotl, who asked if it was safe to ride. Tupac lifted her on the back of his horse, and we started to leave.

Just then a haggard looking young Chiapas woman with desperate hope in her eye grabbed Tupac's leg and said, "Sir, I have been physically and sexually abused in this brutal society. I have had heard about your village and beg you to take me with you because I want to join." While Tupac was pondering her request many more women ran to him and also begged to be taken. After more thought Tupac said "you are welcome to come with us, but I cannot guarantee the tribe will accept you—that is up to them to decide. But I will give you the chance, I will insure your safety, I will try to persuade my village to accept you and, if they don't, I will do my best to find you another place to live in peace." The relieved and grateful women thanked him, ran and gathered their possessions including some children and we all left. On the way out Yaotl emotionally looked back at the Chiapas village and felt tremendous relief that her thirteen-year nightmare was over.

After a while Tupac and Yaotl dismounted and walked together, lagging behind talking and reconnecting. They reminisced about their happy childhood days playing and swimming and their adolescent plans. As they spoke, she reminded Tupac of her cheerful and resilient nature. At one point he asked what had happened to her, and she went quiet but quickly regained her courage. She said, "It was a harrowing experience. When I was captured they roughly tied my hands behind me, put a hood over my head, roped me to a horse and made me walk back to their village. At the village they made me a slave and treated me like an untouchable. I later surmised that I was being saved for special sacrifice at the temple for the Xiuhmolpilli, or new fire festival, which happens every fifty-two years." She said, "I lived in terror knowing my fate." She then said with tears in her eyes, "I was to be sacrificed within the month, but you have saved me."

Then Yaotl noticed the wound in Tupac's shoulder and said, "You have been injured and it is bleeding." Tupac said, "It can wait until we get to the village." Yaotl replied, "No. Sit here." Tupac complied and Yaotl applied a healing herb and re-bandaged it with cloth she had ripped from her skirt. When they started walking again Yaotl asked what Tupac had been doing. He smiled and said, "I have had many challenges and successes." He described his problems with Ati and the caste system and his frustration because he could not be a warrior. He described leaving the old village, founding Esperanza, the bow and arrow, the pumas and the Chiapas attacks. As they walked on in silence Yaotl was thrilled to see Tupac, now a handsome warrior and chief of his village.

When they got just inside the caldera, still behind the others, Yaotl said she wanted to see the old village. Walking in to the ruins was an emotional shock to her as she imagined it in her youth. She ran to the location of her family hut and fell on her knees crying. Suddenly she excitedly asked "Tupac, my parents, are they still alive?" Tupac said, "Yes, they are at Esperanza and you shall see them soon." Suddenly Meztil came galloping in and excitedly said, "We have been followed. Some men have been behind us, and they are not far away!" Tupac immediately mounted and grabbed Yaotl, and the three of them raced to catch up. Near the entrance to Esperanza, Tupac yelled to everyone, "Warriors behind us! Rush to the gate," and let Yaotl down. Just as everyone was in the gate Tupac, Metzil, Izel, Camaxtli and I turned and rode fast to the ravine nearby, stopping at the rim.

We could see there were people in the brush at the bottom but could not make them out. Because it was getting dark and we did not know what we were up against, we decided to return to the village and confront them in the morning. After we rode in they closed the gate and Tupac explained the danger and the presence of the Chiapas women to the curious and alarmed villagers. He then noticed Yaotl obviously overjoyed hugging her parents as they walked off to their home in the distance. We posted some sentries and spent a tense night not sure what to expect.

Early in the morning a sentry sounded an alarm, so we ran to the parapet and saw two fully armored and armed Spaniards surveying our wall. We learned later that they had been foraging and when they saw us decided to follow. When they saw us one raised his arquebus and fired, just missing Camaxtli, so we sent a barrage of arrows at them that just bounced off their armor. With that they abruptly left, and Esperanza slowly returned to normal.

CHAPTER NINE

Yaotl

A few days later Tupac sent me and Izel to see if the Chiapas village was deserted, which it was, but this was the least of his worries. The Spaniards now knew our location and that our arrows are harmless against their armor. Early the next morning he went to check on the arquebus and caldera wall. After he captured the arquebus and learned how to use it with the help of Nacalli, he had started thinking about ways to increase its rate of fire. He had pondered various contraptions like a reloading breach without success. He had an idea and recruited five adolescent boys in the tribe who were quick and strong enough to handle the gun but too young to be warriors. He explained the Spanish threat to them. He told them that the gun might defeat the enemy except that it takes about thirty seconds to reload and fire. This meant only two rounds per minute, which is way too slow. He said, "I want to see if you five can work in tandem to make it fire faster," and the boys enthusiastically said, "Sure!"

Tupac took them to a remote place and with Nacalli's help showed the excited boys how to fire the gun. He added gunpowder to the barrel, inserted the ball, rammed it tight, struck the flint in the priming pan, lit the fuse and aimed it — it went boom! The boys jumped with joy. Carefully watching, he next had each of them fire the weapon. He noticed that Icnoyotl was good with gunpowder, Nahuatl was agile and could quickly insert the ball, strong Tiacelel could ram it tight, Eztli liked the sparking flint and was quick to light the fuse and Ohtil was a deadly shot. Every time the gun went off the boys—being boys—jumped with glee and begged to do it again. With Nacalli watching, Tupac then organized the boys into a firing tag team according to their strengths. They were quite clumsy at first with only one round every thirty to forty seconds.

After a while, Tupac wanted to see if they had improved. He rounded them up, and they adroitly set up the gun. To his amazement, they swiftly shot off twelve rounds in one minute—one every five seconds! They had become so fast and proficient you could hardly see their hands move—they were just a blur. Tupac was amazed and said to the proud boys, "Good job and stay practiced because we will need your teamwork soon." He thought to himself that these young men would make superb future Hidalgo warriors.

He next went to check on the wall to the caldera. In the past he had problems with Tlacelel, the stonemason and builder. Tlacelel was an independent and stubborn man who did most of the work on the wall face himself. One day Tupac had seen him working high up without a safety harness and said, "Tlacelel, wear a harness because if you fall it could be fatal," to which Tlacelel defiantly replied, "I work freely, I don't want a harness." Tupac said, "Wear it or you are off the job, and in a huff Tlacelel left."

As a good leader, Tupac stood his ground, and it did not take long for cooled-off Tlacelel to grudgingly ask Tupac to start work again, agreeing to wear a harness. It was only a couple of days later when he slipped and fell, only to be saved by the harness. He never outwardly thanked Tupac for his good judgment, but you could tell he always held a silent gratitude and reverence for him. So when Tupac arrived, proud Tlacelel greeted him warmly and said, "It is done except the gate." Tupac replied that it was a good job but that we needed to finish the gate quickly because the Spaniards could arrive anytime.

The next event in Tupac's life I am going to tell you is one of my favorites because it is so satisfying and heartwarming. That evening all the villagers were sitting around a bonfire in the common area eating, laughing and enjoying life. Tupac was sitting in the front row talking with Zyanya when Yaotl entered with her parents. She was wearing a white dress with shinning sequins and stunning jeweled necklace. Her hair was coiffured elegantly, flowing and high at the back with a flower over her temple. She was absolutely gorgeous and everyone was stunned with her beauty watching in silence as she went to sit down. Tupac could not take his eyes off her.

We all expected Tupac to go sit with her but uncharacteristically he just sat there for a long time dumbfounded. Finally puzzled Zyanya said to him, "What is your problem, go sit with her." Tupac said that he was scared to death and did not know what to do. He said he did not know much about love and women and feared he would do the wrong thing. It is the only time I ever saw him like a little kid so nervous and indecisive. Zyanya shook her head, took his hand and said, "Come with me." She led him like a puppy dog in front of everyone over to Yaotl. She said, "Yaotl, Tupac wants to sit with you, but he is too shy to ask." Yaotl smiled at Tupac and cleared a place next to her. He sat down.

It did not take long for the two childhood friends to start talking, smiling, laughing and touching one another while everyone watched intently wanting to see what would happen next. It took only two affectionate rubs on the back and kiss on the cheek by Yoatl when the old decisive Tupac I knew suddenly emerged. His face abruptly changed from a scared little boy to a man, he looked long at Yaotl, scanned the eager crowd and got up and walked over to Yaotl's parents. Aloud he told them he loved their daughter and wanted permission to marry her, to which they only smiled and said, "Of course." He then went back to Yaotl, took her by the hand, lead her to the center and got on one knee. He said "Yaotl, I love you. Will you marry me?" She immediately said, "Yes." With that a great cheer went up as the two embraced kissing.

But Tupac was not finished because he was a warrior who got things done. He asked the Sabiduria sitting in the crowd to come and marry them. The atmosphere became solemn as the Sabiduria started leading them through their vows. He finally proclaimed, "I now pronounce you husband and wife." They kissed passionately as he announced to the villagers, "I now present you Tupac and Yatol, husband and wife, chief and queen." Another great cheer went up, and everyone celebrated late into the night.

Tupac and Yaotl disappeared early from the celebration, and when they returned in the morning Yaotl looked beautifully radiant and Tupac worn out, haggard and disheveled — which gave us warriors a good laugh.

It turned out Tupac's love for Yaotl was infectious. I had lived most of my life lamenting the loss of my wife and child. I wanted a family but had resigned myself to my lonely fate. Shortly after Tupac married I told him something I had not told anyone—I felt like an adolescent kid asking for advice from his father. I told Tupac my heart was warmed watching him with Yaotl. I hesitated and then said, "I think I love Tlalli. I used to despise her arrogance, but she is not like that at all. She is humble, kind and one of the hardest workers in the village; she thinks I am handsome. I want to marry her." Then I asked what he thought. Tupac grinned, shook his head, put his hand on my shoulder and said "Aztec, if you love her, what are you waiting for?" Like Tupac, I decided I needed to get things done, so I went straightaway to Tlalli and asked her to marry me. She said yes, and the Sabiduria married us within a week.

I was very happy to be in love and married to Tlalli. She was about forty and I was close to fifty, so you can only imagine my shock when she told me shortly afterward that she was pregnant! I went into immediate shock—I could not believe it. I asked her if she was sure, and she said she was pretty sure. I was absolutely thrilled; I carefully rubbed her tummy and hugged my Tlalli for a very long time. I had thought I would never have a wife, children or family, but now at fifty I did! Later that year, Tlalli gave birth to a healthy baby boy who we named Tupac. It turned out Tupac's infection was quite contagious, because within a week Nicalli proposed to one of the Chiapas women, Mazatl, and married her.

CHAPTER TEN
Spanish Attack

After the Chiapas attack things settled down at Esperanza. Like Tlalli, Yaotl quickly got pregnant—in time she was raising a brood of children with Tupac. Tenoch recovered from his wound, and Tlacelel finished the wall to the caldera. Initially, Tupac had some difficulty getting the new Chiapas women settled. At first they were quite scared; they had difficulty communicating because even though we spoke the same language we used some different words and pronunciations that confused them, so they kept to themselves. Also, some villagers were wary of accepting former enemies into our midst. Tupac decided to enlist the help of some leading village women, so he asked his mother, Zuma, Patli, Tenoch and Tlalli to help. He told them how they had been abused in their old village and how much they wanted to join ours.

The women were sympathetic with their plight so they took up the challenge. They assigned each one of the group to two Chiapas women and started teaching them our language, describing our ways, giving them meaningful work and introducing them to everyone. It did not take long for the villagers to see how hard they worked, how eager they were to help and how pleasant they were. Over time they earned everyone's respect and with joy and gratitude in their hearts were accepted into the tribe. Most of them married Hidalgo men and started families.

Things suddenly changed one day when a sentry sent up an alarm from the caldera wall.

When we got there we saw what looked like the same two Spanish men that had earlier surveyed the village wall now studying our caldera wall and gate. When they saw us they again quickly got on their horses and rode away. This concerned us because it looked like they were figuring out how to attack us and had gone to get others. There had been persistent ominous rumors that a Spaniard called Conquistador Cortes and his army were systematically attacking villages and subduing indigenous people. It was said that they wore heavy armor, rode horses and carried fire sticks, which we now knew were arquebuses, that killed from a distance. Our primitive weapons were useless against them. It was said they were invincible.

It turned out Tlacelel finished the gate just in time because within two days about fifty fearsome looking Spaniards arrived. The alarm was raised around midday so we collected our weapons and everyone ran to the caldera wall. We saw a new kind of armored enemy that was calmly and methodically going about the dirty business of trying to conquer us. They had brought a large log suspended on a wheeled cart that they were using to batter down our gate. Like the Chiapas raid, Tupac wanted to lull them into a sense of security, so he had us send a hail of arrows that wounded a few but mostly bounced off their armor. With that the Spaniards unleashed a hail of bullets that ricocheted everywhere injuring Izel and killing one citizen solider—it was like nothing I had ever experienced—it was like fifty invisible and lethal hornets whizzing around my head. Then, while some continued to fire at us others resumed smashing our gate, which was beginning to shatter and give way.

Just as they were about to break through Tupac yelled "Fire," and we threw everything we had at them. The eager tag team of Icnoyotl, Nahuatl, Tiacelel, Eztli and Ohtil started furiously firing the arquebus at one round every five seconds, the warriors sent volley after volley of arrows into their mist, Zyanya started picking them off with her well-placed arrows hitting their exposed legs and necks and everyone else started throwing spears at them. They were stunned as bullets penetrated their armor — they did not know what hit them. They stopped battering the gate but kept up their fire; we kept up ours also and slowly began thinning their ranks. They managed to get through a hole in the gate so Tupac, Meztil and I ran to meet the challenge, which quickly turned into hand-to-hand combat. As more of them poured through, the fight became more vicious. We were a few against many strong armored men with their unusually long swords, but then Tupac took over. Once again the warrior spirit seized him like it had done against the Chiapas and his sword sang. He quickly killed three Spaniards and the others fled. He was a joy to watch — I was glad a spirit was on my side.

Just then through the gate Tupac saw one of them stand and waive a white flag so he called for Nacalli and asked what that means. Nacalli said it means they want a truce and to talk. The Spaniard with the flag and now no helmet approached alone so Tupac went out to meet him along with nervous Nacalli who interpreted. All firing stopped as the big, imposing Spaniard looked long and hard at Tupac and finally said, "You are quite an opponent, you must have some Spanish blood." Obviously impressed with Tupac's fierce warrior presence he said, "My name is Conquistador Cortes, I have conquered over twenty of your villages, but now I have an arrow in my thigh, I have lost half of my men and I have never encountered such a fierce tribe as yours." Tupac said nothing so Cortes continued: "It appears I can't beat you, so I would like to discuss peace."

Tupac was obviously weary of the stranger as the two of them stood for a long time in the open talking and sizing each other up. We could not hear them, but Nacalli later told us what happened. He said Cortez first did not discuss peace but repeatedly asked if we had any gold. He talked on the importance of bringing Catholicism and the Holy Ghost to our village. Tupac replied that we had no gold and are pantheists. Tupac had always been a good judge of character and quickly surmised Cortes was an avaricious man who believed in spirits. Watching in disbelief, Nacalli said then Tupac went face to face with Cortes and said in Spanish "Cortes, I am a warrior spirit from the past in the body of a man sent here to protect this Hidalgo tribe. I have killed many beasts and men who have tried to harm them, and if you harm them I will kill you too." Nacalli said Cortes's face went white with fear after being threatened by a warrior spirit who spoke perfect Spanish with a royal accent.

With that they agreed to peace and shook hands, and Cortes and the remaining Spaniards left.

CHAPTER ELEVEN

Esperanza

So, that is the remarkable story of Tupac. Cortes went on to conquer our countrymen but was good to his word and left us alone—the Hidalgo tribe was the only one to remain intact. Years later after Cortes had become famous we learned that he had been told about the arquebus tag team and Zyanya and one of his favorite stories was about the only time he was ever defeated. Amused he would say it was by a warrior spirit named Tupac helped by five adolescent boys and young girl with a deformed arm.

I have told you this story with great joy in my heart. I was once dispirited living in the Chiapas tribe and then the old Hidalgo village that was dying but that all changed when Tupac ascended. With his leadership we defeated our old enemies, the pumas and Chiapas, and new one, the Spanish. Our village is now safe and free from external threat. The old village's depressing miasmic fear has been replaced with a new optimistic and vibrant spirit eager for challenges and progress. With Tupac's vision we built the best village with baths and showers and forged new liberating norms and laws, changing the role of women, eliminating castes and rewarding merit. Tupac also changed for the better how we are governed and created a new tolerant and comforting religion without sacrifices.

Unlike the old village, Esperanza is regenerating. Past generations may have passed, including Tupac and Yaotl's parents, but a new vital generation is on its way. Tupac, Yaotl, their old childhood friends Zuma and Meztil; Patli and Izel, who recovered from his wound; and Yaretzi and Tenoch along with Zyanya and Cualli and many of the married Chiapas women are busy raising children. The young adolescent arquebus tag team of Icnoyotl, Nahuatl, Tiacelel, Eztli and Ohtil are rapidly growing into our new generation of strong young warriors. They are eager, bright, full of fun and spirit, optimistic, thoughtful, kind and brave. That insures Esperanzo's future. They worship Tupac like a spirit who passed on his characteristics to them and future generations of Hidalgo men.

Over the years I had many deep conversations with Tupac that gave me insight into his spiritually inspired philosophies of life. There were many, but I think there were three significant ones. The first is to ignore the oppressive norms of society and opinions of other people. Norms like the former caste system of the old village make you a bird in a cage with an open door afraid to fly to freedom. Likewise the thoughts of others, like the old chief Ati's stubborn unwillingness to make Tupac a warrior, can become your mental prison. Strive to be the best you can be whatever that is. The second is to solve your life problems with your brain. Tupac faced many problems in his life, including pumas, Chiapas and Spaniards, but he figured out ways to defeat them, whether it is with a bow and arrow, horses, rapid-fire arquebuses or with his mind. He believed overcoming problems in a thoughtful, peaceful way was better than violently by force — he only used force when he had no alternative. Perhaps his greatest belief was to have courage. He said that nothing changes if you don't try. He once told me he thought it was a shame that so many people prefer to remain in misery with their fears than face unknown and perhaps worse possible futures. He believed people must summon the courage to face their daemons and fulfill their futures. I think he was a profound voice from the ages.

Tupac was special and my hunch about him being our tribe's savoir was right. He turned out to be the bravest, wisest and greatest philosopher chief the tribe ever had. He was a gift from the ages, a warrior spirit out of time. The spirit had picked a situation requiring a warrior, choosing one strong individual who himself was facing troubles to represent the spirit to save the tribe, and it chose Tupac, our great warrior chief.